On th

Contents **Page**

written by Pam Holden

What do sheep have on the outside?

They have wool on the outside.
wool

What do fish have
on the outside?

They have scales
on the outside.

What do dogs have on the outside?
Dogs have hair on the outside.

hair

What do hedgehogs
have on the outside?

They have prickles on the outside.

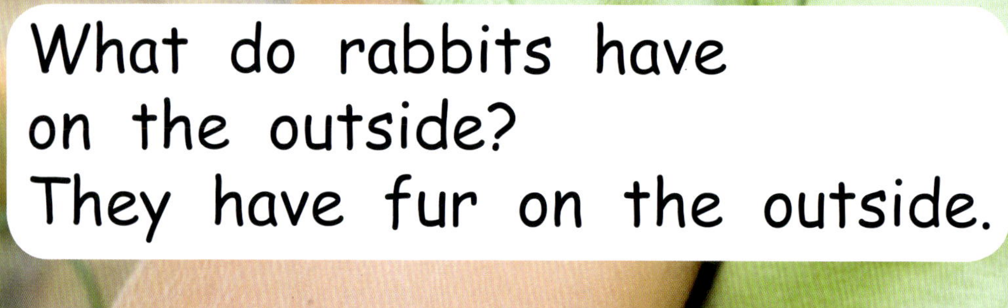
What do rabbits have
on the outside?
They have fur on the outside.

fur

What do snails have
on the outside?
Snails have shells
on the outside.

shell

What do birds have on the outside?

They have feathers
on the outside.

clothes

What do people have on the outside?
People have clothes!